GLOSSARY

Anemometer A device that measures the speed of wind.

Atmosphere The layer of air around the Earth, which becomes less dense with height.

Atom The smallest piece or particle of a pure substance (chemical element).

Barometer A device that measures the pressure of air.

Density The amount of matter of a substance, usually measured as mass or weight, in a certain volume.

Drag The force pushing against an object as it travels through a fluid, as when air pushes back on a car.

Fluid A substance that can flow, including liquids like water, and gases like those in air.

Gas A substance that can flow, and which can change volume to fill its container completely.

Isobar The line on a weather map that joins places of equal atmospheric pressure.

Kinetic energy The energy possessed by an object or substance due to its having movement or motion.

Lift A force created by the wing shape called the aerofoil, which lifts a plane upwards.

Meteorology The study of the atmosphere, especially the processes and events of weather and climate.

Molecules Two or more atoms joined together, to make the smallest pieces or particles of most everyday substances and materials.

Pressure Pushing or pressing force measured over a certain area.

Thermometer A device that measures temperature, or the amount of heat energy in a substance or object.

Wind resistance The force pushing against an object that tries to move through air or against the wind.

Wind vane A broad surface that can swivel around, to show the direction in which the wind blows.

FOR ALL MY SOUTH AFRICAN FRIENDS, ESPECIALLY SAM, WHO INTRODUCED ME TO THE STORY.

— ALAN DURANT

FOR MY WONDERFUL WIFE, KEEGAN BLANKENAAR AND PIET GROBLER — THIS BOOK WOULD BE IMPOSSIBLE WITHOUT YOU.

— DALE BLANKENAAR

FOR THE PROTECTION AND CONSERVATION OF THE ENDANGERED ANIMALS IN THIS BOOK.

— TINY OWL

First published in the UK in 2019 by
Tiny Owl Publishing, London

TINY OWL

For thousands of years, people have been telling stories.
From this rich global heritage, we can find stories that are
strikingly similar but also different. *One Story, Many Voices*
explores well-known stories from all over the world.
For teacher resources and more information, visit
www.tinyowl.co.uk

#QuillSoup

#OneStoryManyVoices

A catalogue record for this book is available from the British Library.

ISBN 978-1-910328-40-8

Printed in Malta

FSC
www.fsc.org

MIX
Paper from
responsible sources
FSC® C022612

QUILL
SOUP

Alan Durant
Dale Blankenaar

Noko the porcupine was hungry and tired.
He'd been travelling through the Valley of a
Thousand Hills and hadn't eaten for days.

He saw a small village ahead and his spirits lifted.
"Food and shelter at last," he thought.

Meanwhile in the village, the animals caught sight of Noko.
"There's a stranger coming!" squeaked Monkey.

"Quick, run to your homes!"
shouted Meerkat.

Noko trudged into the village.
It was silent and empty.

"Hello, friends!" he called.
But there was no reply.

Noko went to the first house and tapped on the door.

"Yes?" said Warthog.

"I've travelled a long way and I'm very hungry," said Noko.

"Do you have anything I can eat?"

Warthog shook her big head.

"I'm sorry," she replied. "I ate a big lunch and all my food is gone."

Noko knocked at the next house.

"How can I help?" asked Rabbit.

"Please, I need some food," said Noko.

"So do I!" Rabbit exclaimed.
"My greedy brother came to visit
and ate all my food. I have nothing left."

Noko knocked at Monkey's door.

"Yes, what is it?" Monkey asked.

"I wonder if you have any food to spare a poor traveller?" Noko inquired.

"We are *poor* villagers," Monkey grumbled. "We don't have any spare food."

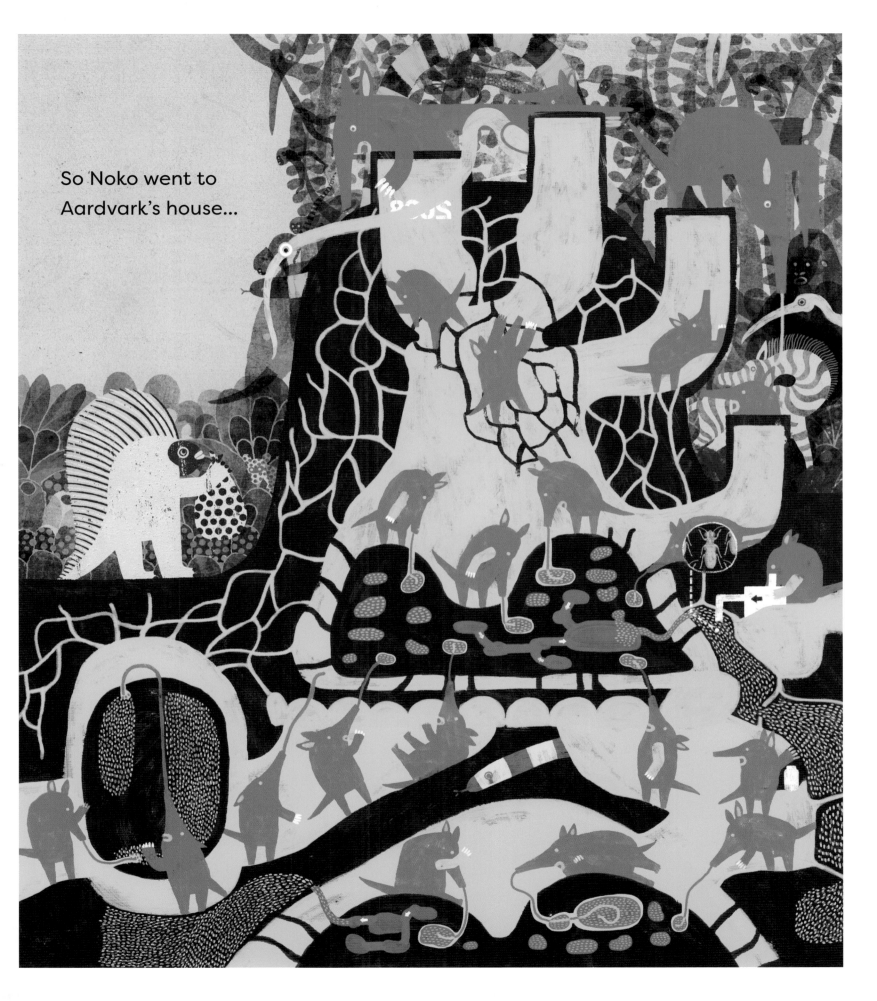

So Noko went to
Aardvark's house...

and Meerkat's house...

and Pangolin's house.

But he came away hungry. None of them, they said, had any food.

By this time Noko was very tired and very hungry indeed.
But his brain was as sharp as the quills on his back.

He could see from the villagers' sleek coats
and rounded bellies that they were lying.

He knew they had food. But how was he going to get some?

He sat and thought, and after a while
he came up with a plan.

"I wonder if I might have a little fire and a large
pot of water," he asked the villagers.

"Of course," they replied.
They couldn't refuse him that.

2071

Noko put the pot on the fire to boil.

"It seems I shall have to make my own food."
He sighed. "I shall make quill soup."

He plucked three quills from his back and
dropped them into the pot.

2067

"But surely the quills are too hard and sharp to eat," Warthog said.

"Wait and see! Soon they will soften and release their flavour to make a delicious soup," Noko explained.

He bent over the pot and dipped in his paw.
Then he licked it and nodded.

"*Mmmm*, tasty," he said.
"Just how His Majesty likes it."

2067

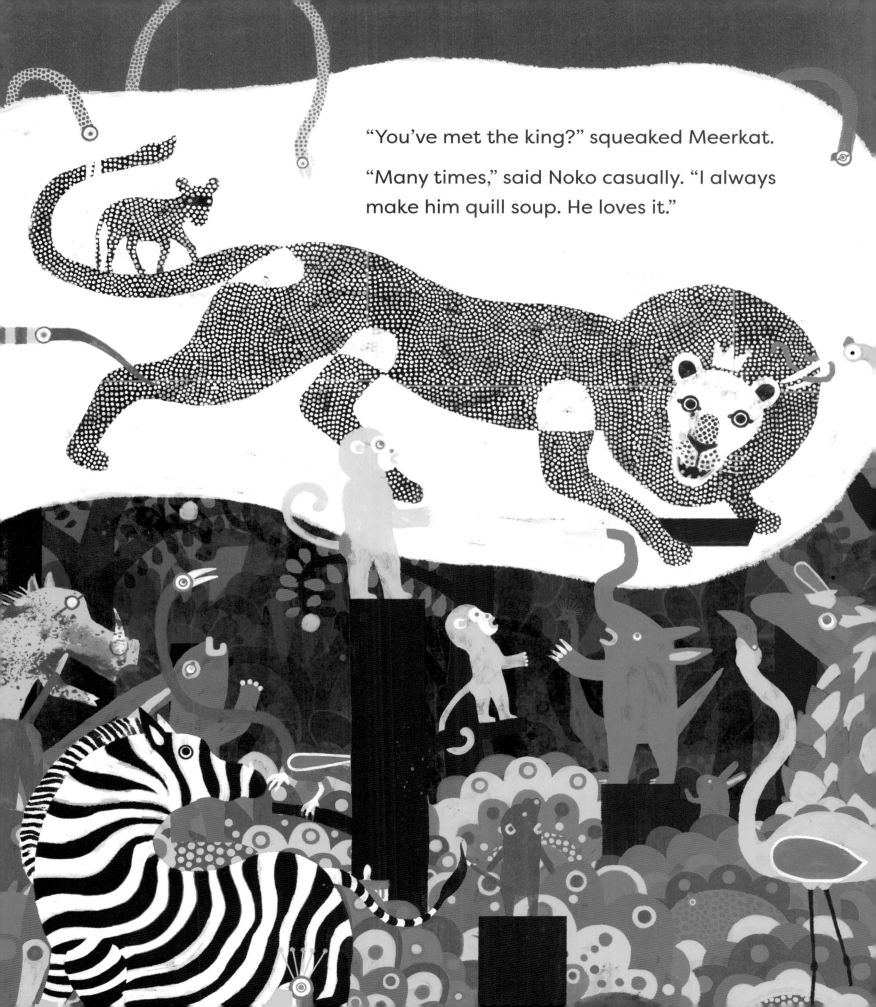

"You've met the king?" squeaked Meerkat.

"Many times," said Noko casually. "I always make him quill soup. He loves it."

Noko tasted the soup again.

"If only I had some carrots..." he said ruefully.

2067

Rabbit's ears shot up. He wanted to taste quill soup that was fit for a king.

"I think my greedy brother may have left a carrot or two," he blurted and he hopped away to fetch them.

Noko added the carrots to the water and tasted the soup again.

"Lovely," he announced. "Of course, the king likes mealies in his quill soup..."

"I've got mealies!" squealed Meerkat and she ran away to find them.

Each time Noko tasted the soup, there was something
that needed to be added: beans, peas, potatoes, spinach...
In moments, as if by magic, all these things appeared.

Now Noko's soup was thick and rich.
Once again he tasted it.

"Perfect," he declared,
"unless... I don't suppose
anyone has a few worms?"

Pangolin did!

2067

Noko told the villagers to fetch their bowls.
"There's plenty of soup to share," he said.

And share they did! They drank bowl after
bowl of the delicious soup in the firelight
until the big pot was empty.

Noko sat back, looked up at the stars,
and yawned.

"I wonder if you might have a hole
where I could sleep?" he asked.

"A hole!" cried Monkey. "For our friend who
has cooked delicious quill soup for the king?"

"And who has the generosity to share it
with strangers?" piped Aardvark.

"No, my friend," said Monkey.
"You, Noko, shall have the very best bed
in my house."

"You're too kind," Noko smiled.

2067

Before they went to their beds, Noko and the villagers sang together, shared stories and danced in the moonlight.

And later with a full tummy and a happy heart,
Noko the traveller went to sleep at last.

GOODNIGHT!